The Witches of Raven Hollow

Raymond G. Newsome

<u>Chapter One</u>

Flames crackled in the fireplace heating the cauldron to its boiling point. Red embers disappeared up the chimney. The fallen leaves in the yard reflected a haunting reality of harsher, colder weather. A soft voice hummed from a rocking chair on the porch. Agatha swung her head in rhythm with the chair's movement. She continued her sweet song until approaching horses snapped her out of a trance.

"Where is your mother, child?" The man stared down from his saddle. His hat revealed little above his mouth. Stubble clung to his chin and jawline.

"Are you my Papa?"

"What's that?"

"You don't look like my Papa. Why should I tell you anything?" Agatha kept her eyes locked on the grass under the animals.

"How dare you, you little-" The second man's words ended as the leader raised his hand.

Agatha smirked. "You have a lovely pet."

The second man cursed unsettling his horse for a second. His boss interrupted once again. "I'll ask you one more time. Where is your mother? My name is Williams. We have an arrangement."

"Mama is inside with my sisters."

"Will you fetch her?"

"She's waiting for you inside." She paused for a minute for the pair to dismount. "You have to go alone. No spares are allowed."

"Wait here, Patterson." The leader nodded at his partner, who whispered another curse. A hand patted the child's head. He slipped through the door leaving the other man with Agatha. The horses swayed nervously.

Agatha felt Patterson's anxiety rise higher since she separated the pair. She returned to her song humming to herself. A smile flickered on her lips. The rocking chair stopped. Her song ended on a quiet note. Agatha stared at the man she called a pet.

He realized the child stared at him. "What's the matter, brat?"

"I wanted to listen to his screams." She sat still enough to hear both of their heartbeats. Her concentration broke when Patterson adjusted his weight on the worn saddle. She glanced back toward the front door.

"Who's screams?" Condensation appeared on his brow, sweat from the heat or panic.

"Your boss." She smiled at the man. She watched him physically shake before he slid from his saddle.

"What are you talking about?" Patterson mounted the step leading up to the porch when his partner's screams echoed through the house. He froze in his tracks. A quivering hand reached for the pistol in his holster.

"I wouldn't bother with that, mister," she said. The smile taunted the grown man, yet she refused to avert her eyes.

"What the hell are you talking about?" He pointed the gun at the little girl in the rocking chair.

"You have your own devils coming for you." Agatha dropped from her seat. She stepped forward until the barrel pressed against her forehead.

"Listen, you little bitch! I'll kill you!"

Agatha's eyes were ice cold. "Kill me? You're already dead."

Vines tightened around Patterson's throat. The pistol fell into Agatha's hands as he thrashed for freedom. More vines secured his arms and legs. The man's body slammed to the ground spooking the horses. A scream for its way out of his throat before it was cut off. Leafy strands slithered into his open mouth. Patterson continued flailing with fear of the inevitable feeding his adrenaline. His body stopped its battle when a bullet pierced his head.

Agatha walked into the house carrying the pistol. She followed whispering voices to the kitchen. Her mother and sisters sat at a table discussing the plans for the bodies. Agatha heard a moan come from the corner.

The other victim, Williams, dangled from the rafters by his ankles. His clothes lay tattered on the floor in a heap. Sections of flesh had been peeled away from his body. Blood dripped into a wooden tub.

"What was that sound, Agatha?" her mother asked.

"I shot him. I got tired of his wriggling." She laid the gun on the table.

"Where is he now?"

"He's with Mother Earth. May I go to bed now?"

"Yes, go to bed. I prefer the three of you to go. I'll be up when I finish in here."

"Yes, Mama," the three girls said in unison, sounding so innocent.

They slipped out of the room after giving her a kiss on the cheek. In a single file, they climbed the stairs to their beds. Agatha closed her eyes listening to the insects sing their nightly song.

Downstairs, their mother walked to the corner where Williams hung upside down. She examined the man. His groan drifted into a soft murmur with the growing hallucinations from blood loss. He talked to the empty space about their plans to kill the hag and her brats. She listened to his idea of luring them out before shooting them in the head. Everything he planned so they did not have to pay for their services.

Mother stroked his wet, sticky face. "You poor, delusional man. I knew your plan the entire time. The ravens told me."

She stood up walking over to a knife in her sink. "The ravens will feast on your carcass as my offering."

Williams sobbed quietly. He felt his tears as they ran down his forehead. The man watched the witch drop to her knees in front of him. She raised the knife to his left eye. Williams pressed his eyelids closed tight.

Mother paused with a frown on her face. She placed a hand on her hip. "Now stop being a child. You brought this on yourself."

The knife plunged through Williams' left eyelid. He attempted a scream until something grabbed his throat squeezing his windpipe. The witch carved his eye out of its socket while the thing maintained its grip. He refused to open his last eye despite fingers attempting to pry it. He knew he would die. Nothing could stop him from giving up one more fight.

A cold breath on his face sent a chill through his being. He felt a hand similar to the one gripping his throat make its way up to his dangling body. Fingers traveled through his chest hair reaching up. It found its destination with a hold on his manhood.

The sudden pleasure overpowered his pain. A tongue licked him hard.

Williams heard a soft voice whisper in his ear as a hand rubbed on him. The other released his throat. "Look at me, James."

"I can't. She's going to cut out my other eye."

Another soft sensual lick brought a moan to his lips. "I want you to see me before you're no longer able."

"Oh, okay." He peered into a pair of mesmerizing golden eyes.

It kissed him seductively causing most of his body to relax. He felt his excitement build closer to release. The eyes closed as it whispered again.

"Do you think I'm beautiful, James?"

"Yes, I do." He blinked.

The face moved further away morphing into something grotesque. Its skin looked covered in scales. A tail whipped around behind it. It leaned its mouth to his ear. "Do you still find me beautiful, James?"

"Yes, I do." He repeated after a brief pause.

"You're lying to me, James." The succubus's free hand clutched his throat. "Do it."

Mother leaned forward with a grin on her face. "With pleasure."

Mother placed the knife into his right eye socket removing the gelatinous orb. She held the pair of eyeballs in her hand turning to add them to her collection in the large Mason jar on the table. She sat down watching the succubus.

"I'll give you the pleasure of finishing him off."

The succubus winked at Mother. She licked him wrapping her tail around his neck. She used it to pull his face closer to her crotch. She sucked on him hard bringing him to an end. She rubbed against his mouth and chin for her personal pleasure tightening the grip on his neck.

"Do you think I'm beautiful, James?" The tail dug further into his skin until it dropped into the small pool of blood.

Mother stood up moving for the kitchen doorway. "I ask you to dispose of him somewhere the ravens can find the body."

"As you wish. Will you have a new plaything for me soon?"

"The full moon comes in a fortnight. I'm sure we will have plenty of company within that time."

The succubus clapped her hands. "I can't wait."

"Goodnight. I'll summon you soon." Mother joined her daughter upstairs letting the night's events fade into a distant memory. She kissed each girl on the forehead before settling into bed. Mother closed her eyes and drifted off to sleep.

<u>Chapter Two</u>

The Byrne family woke with the morning light. Three girls huddled under their blankets while their mother summoned fire in the fireplace. She lit a flame in the kitchen stove so breakfast could be prepared.

Mother used her ladle to scoop water into the old teapot placing it on the stove. She dug through the cupboard for any remaining smoked meat. They had plenty stored in the smokehouse, but she hoped to wait until they finished breakfast. The woman opened the curtains for the morning sunlight. Mother found the sitting room warm enough for her daughters to join her downstairs.

Agatha yawned. Her arms reached for the clouds in mid-stretch. A hand-me-down nightgown hung to her ankles. At eight years old, she was the youngest of the Byrne sisters. Agatha curled up in a chair resting her head on the arm. "Mama, is breakfast ready?"

"Not yet, my beloved. The water is on the stove for tea. I'm about to start cooking." Mother called from the kitchen table.

She examined her herbs growing in the window sill. A cabinet in the corner held her store of dried herbs. Herbs she used for cooking and spells. The deadliest plants of her collection were in a small box on top of the cabinet. Her attention moved to the empty basket on the table.

"Cora, be sure to check the hen house for eggs. I know yesterday was exciting, but it's your chore to collect the eggs."

"Yes, Mama." She reached for her coat and boots by the door.

"Alice, bring in any firewood left by the house inside. We'll gather more later, the four of us."

"Yes, Mama." Alice followed her sister outside.

Agatha sprung for her chair for the kitchen. "What can I do, Mama?"

"You can have a seat at the table while we wait for your older sisters. I need you to save your energy for our trip into the woods later. We're out of firewood so we need as much as possible to keep us through the approaching winter. I believe we'll have to spend the next few days gathering."

Agatha watched her mother place the venison in their only copper pan. The strips sizzled. Agatha heard the door open with Cora holding it for Alice. Alice dropped her first load of wood by the fireplace. Cora emptied her pockets into the basket on the table. She received a kiss on her head for her effort. Without a word, she slipped out to help her sister finish her chore.

Eggs landed in the hot pan once Mother removed the venison strips. She maneuvered the eggs, so they fried on each side. Four plates sat on the table with eggs and venison. Tea steamed gently out of four cups. Mother looked up at Agatha.

"Aggie, can you get the leftover cornbread by the washbasin."

"Yes, Mama." Agatha jumped up rushing for the pan. She packed it to the table doing her best to reach the middle.

Mother took the cornbread placing it between the plates. She heard her oldest daughters walk into the kitchen. "Breakfast is ready my darlings."

The girls sat down breaking a piece of cornbread in half to share with their mother and sister. A quiet, cool autumn morning made their meager warm meal all the more welcome. Ravens landed on the window sill with a warning caw. Mother stopped eating walking through the house to the front door.

Horses approached the house emerging from the woods. Agatha stood at the window watching the posse come closer. She rolled her eyes rushing to the table so she could finish her cooling eggs. Her sisters concentrated on their plates not giving a second look to the sounds outside.

Mother opened the door standing in the frame with her arms crossed. "May I help you, gentlemen?"

The leader rode up to the porch. "Lady Byrne, two men rode out to see you yesterday. They never returned to town. Do you know what became of them?"

"They paid a visit then they left our property the same way they arrived. I've no idea what happened to them once they crossed into the woods."

"Their horses returned without any riders. We've searched for them high and low. No one has found them."

"I'm sad to hear that. Mister Williams was a good customer. I hate to lose his business. I hope they're safe and sound."

The man studied her for a moment. He nodded turning his horseback to the trail. His posse followed him toward the woods. Lady Byrne watched them ride away holding her pose in the doorway.

A raven landed on the railing of the porch. It gave a soft caw from the railing. Lady Byrne nodded. "I want you to keep an eye on them. If they become too curious, make sure the wolves find them."

The bird drifted into the sky surrounded by more. They floated after the posse like a dark cloud. A low menacing energy whistled with the wind. Lady Byrne listened to its song before returning to her children. Slow, deliberate steps toward the kitchen letting the new information flow through her mind.

"What does all that mean, Mama?" Agatha scratched her plate with a fork.

She kissed her youngest daughter on the head then settled in her chair. "It means they suspect us of murdering the men who came to murder us yesterday. In every event, they will find an excuse to come back to murder us."

Agatha followed her mother's beckon climbing in her lap. "What are we going to do?"

"We're going to get ready and collect firewood for the winter."

"What if they come back?"

"We'll finish off anyone who escapes the ravens. Do you understand?"

"Yes, Mama," three sisters replied.

"Good. Help me with the dishes, so we can use the precious sunlight to its fullest extent."

Agatha kicked leaves around with her galoshes skipping between the trees. Cora tapped branches with a small stick trying to keep count. Alice hushed her sisters to hear their mother's song. Lady Byrne hummed a little prayer to her extended family. The oaks and the sycamores and the walnuts and the pines all whispered back.

The Byrnes worked close to their home for their first couple of trips. They packed bundles of kindling and small logs; anything their arms could carry. A stack grew next to the house in slow progression proving their determination. The women of the woods rushed home when the ravens returned with a haunting call.

"Get inside now!" Mother demanded pushing the children through the door.

Three sets of eyes peaked past the window sill. A cyclone of black birds blocked the path leading to the house's front porch. An endless screech pierced the air forcing their young hands to cover their ears. Agatha squeezed her eyes shut. She missed the chaos outside.

Lady Byrne opened her mouth to the trespassing men. Their intent radiated like rattlesnakes perched on their shoulders. She released a horrific shriek forcing the horses to toss each rider. Ravens spun around them with hungry fervor. Her volume reached an excruciating new level leaving her attackers bleeding in pain.

Blood poured from their ears. It streamed from tear ducts and nasal passages. Unknown aneurysms appeared and burst within their brains causing hemorrhages.

The men bled to death in less than a moment. When the ravens ended their dark dance, each corpse had disappeared.

"Girls, I need you now." Mother stood in the grass and autumn leaves. "We have to block every possible path. More will come. They will kill us all if they make it through. We have to protect ourselves."

Hands joined in a circle; four quiet voices called out to their ancestors for help. Vines wove through the trees interlocking their tendrils into a thickening wall. When the spell ended, Agatha spun around staring at their protection and prison. The barrier surrounded the entire property.

"Mama, what happens when vines die?"

"I'll make sure we're ready. For the time, we must remain here. The ravens will provide for us. The forest knows our needs. We will survive until they come for us."

Lady Byrne watched her children return to the warmth of their home. Something grazed the back of her legs.

Mother recognized the familiar touch. Her eyes remained locked on the house.

"You didn't save me anyone to play with, my Lady." The succubus let her lower lip protrude.

"I do apologize. I had little time to prepare. We barely made it in the circle." She surrendered to the monster's touch. A nail traced her back and arms.

"Who will I play with now?"

"Wait until my girls are asleep. You can come to my bed tonight. I'll find you a new playmate soon." Mother walked toward the porch.

"I hope it's someone I can keep alive for a while. They're tastier when I can keep them for a few days or weeks." The succubus vanished with the growing shadows.

Wood crackled with a fire's embrace. New smells filled the rooms flowing from the kitchen, also full of voices. Mother saw her daughters working together

to prepare a stew. She sat down at the table
enjoying their camaraderie. They would
need each other for any hope of survival.

Chapter Three

Shadows reached for the house beneath the moon's light. Lady Byrne stood before the window full of the sky's illumination. She ignored the sound of her visitor's tail making a light tap on the blanket. Her gown slipped off each shoulder to the floor.

Mother felt a hand slide up her back caressing her shoulder and right arm. Gooseflesh spread across the exposed skin like wildfire. The creature's lips lingered near an ear. "What form would you like me to take tonight?"

"Do what you want. I'm here for your pleasure. I ruined your chance for fun earlier. I'm paying the debt for my failure."

"I wish you wouldn't think of it in that way." The succubus kissed the woman's neck. "I enjoy everything much more when my partner falls into the waves of building gratification with me."

Lady Byrne turned toward her magical lover of the night meeting its lips.

Kisses consumed her body with her falling on the mattress as the being changed on top of her. Lady Byrne closed her eyes letting the succubus draw her into an hour of bliss. She gripped the wooden frame with the first of several moans escaping her mouth.

A chill woke Mother in the middle of the night. Her visitor left with the witching hour. She drifted off to sleep in an empty bed. The night's song vanished behind closed eyes and dreamless hours. Mother's newfound awareness brought the realization her blanket had not covered her nakedness. She curled up in the handmade quilt sinking back in the abyss.

Daylight grew. Warmth traveled through the house. A fire crackled downstairs, and the scents of breakfast floated into her room. Mother wandered to the front room where the wood lay stacked neatly beside the fireplace. She heard her girls laughing in the kitchen. Aggie sat in her chair at the table.

Agatha noticed their mother approach from the living room where she rushed to hug her. "Mama, you're finally awake! I'm glad you joined us for breakfast. Cora and Alice cooked for us, Mama."

"Have they? Well, that is wonderful. I apologize for my slow rise. I had a long night." Lady Byrne joined them at the table.

Alice shared a look of concern with Cora for a second being more knowledgeable than their younger sister. She filled their mother's plate and settled into her chair. Alice kept her mouth closed about her worries at breakfast. Her hope of catching a moment with Mother hung in the back of the throat for when the other two had a distraction.

The eldest of the three, Alice, planned to offer herself up to Mother and her succubus as an alternative. She knew Mother had to stand in as the recipient of the creature's lust when a sacrifice could not be found. Alice could not let her mother continue.

Her mother caught her attention with a sharp glance giving her head an adamant shake. The eldest daughter pressed her brows together in frustration. She pleaded with her eyes to have her offer heard. Mother returned to her plate without further expression.

Agatha bounced on her chair waiting for the others to finish. The words clung to the roof of her mouth like dried sap on tree bark. She pressed her lips together tightly as the excitement filled every fiber. The chair squeaked on the wooden floorboards.

"Don't forget to practice your calm, Aggie."

"I'm sorry, Mama. I'll do better."

"I'm sure you can help Cora with some chores after breakfast. We need several things finished this morning." Mother scraped up the remainder of the eggs on her plate.

Cora opened her mouth in protest when Mother stopped her with a shake of her head. She turned her eyes to Alice so Cora would understand they were preparing for a conversation. Cora nodded without a word. She walked her plate to the sink waving Agatha behind her.

Agatha hopped from the chair following her sister with all the speed her legs could muster. The excitement swelled through her body again. Mother wanted her to help with the chores for once. Aggie was over the moon with the chance at responsibility.

She slipped into her hand-me-down boots and coat, of which the latter contained more patches than original leather, following her sister outside. The morning chill left its sting on her cheeks and nose. Agatha ignored the growing sensation in her face too thrilled for the chance to join in.

She looked up to Cora. "What are we doing first?"

"We don't have anything to do. I helped Alice finish everything before breakfast." Cora led the march toward the chicken coop.

"So why did Mama send us out to do chores?" She kept on Cora's heels stopping next to her and peered through the wood planks.

"Alice wanted to talk to her privately about something important. She might have not known we were done for the morning."

"What did Alice have to say?"

"Don't worry about it. You're too young to know."

Agatha crossed her arms letting her lower lip protrude. "I hate it when you say that."

"It's the truth. I promise when you're old enough I'll explain it to you." Cora leaned against the small shed. Her head dropped back as far as it could go next to the wood. She stood there with her eyes closed.

"It still isn't fair." Aggie held her stance.

"You're not the only one who is stuck outside unable to join in their conversation. Don't forget that, Aggie."

Alice exhaled slowly readying her speech. She clasped her hands together to steady their shaking. Her mouth opened, but her voice failed her.

"You're not taking my place with the Succubus, Alice. I forbid it from happening."

"Look how long it took you to recover this morning, Mama. You won't be able to satisfy her forever when we have no one to offer. What if she decides to draw the life force from you more than necessary? We've both seen her drain full-grown men to their deaths for the sheer pleasure. I'm younger. I can recover better."

"It is not your place to satisfy her. It's my contract with Agrat. I have to fulfill it. I refuse to discuss the matter any further."

"Mama, please! I don't want to lose you." Tears welled in Alice's eyes. She squeezed her hands tighter as the tension and pain saturated every muscle.

"I know you're worried, but it is my burden. I shall bear it for as long as I'm capable. After my death, the contract becomes null. You won't see the Succubus once I'm gone." She reached over kissing her eldest daughter's head. Lady Byrne carried their plates to the sink washing them.

The woman used the opportunity to recover from her overwhelming emotions. It was a combination of pride in the strength of her daughter and the fear in the truth of her words. Lady had never slept so late after a night with her friend. She may lose her life eventually, but her children would be free of the succubus's contract.

Alice hugged her mother with her arms wrapped around the woman's waist. The daughter's tear-stained cheek lay against her back. Alice released her hold and went out the door to join her sisters. She knew then they would be her sole focus.

Lady Byrne's pride swelled once more for her daughter's strength. She knew the three of them would always be strong together. Something rubbed the back of her calf.

"You would deny me your daughter when she was willing to offer herself?" The succubus pressed her lips to Lady Byrne's ear. "You should have listened to her."

The succubus kissed Lady hard pulling her remaining life force out of her body and letting it drop to the floor. "Your contract is finished, you selfish woman. Now you can rot in peace knowing you stopped me from getting to them too."

<u>Chapter Four</u>

Alice returned to the kitchen moments later leaving her sisters outside next to the woodpile. She stifled the building sobs in her throat behind a sigh. Turning away, she marched upstairs for the sheet from her mother's bed as a shroud for the empty vessel on the floor. Alice's eyes fixed intently on the corpse, which gradually floated in the air. She released the sheet watching it wrapping around the levitating object of her affection.

A knock came from the main door distracting Alice to the point of dropping the body an inch from the floor. Cora led their sister to stand next to the fireplace. She paused before reaching the scene not wanting to accept the truth. Both girls froze when a small voice came from behind Cora in the middle of the front room.

"Mama's dead, isn't she?" Aggie asked never looking up from the flames.

Cora burst into tears, and Alice squeezed her shoulder while leading the way back to their youngest sibling. Alice leaned down to Aggie. "She is gone. How did you know?"

"She was there in the flames whispering." She pointed to the bright embers.

"What did she say?"

"She said that she loved us and avoid the name of *her*." Young Agatha's face turned grim and serious.

Alice averted her eyes. A plan had begun formulating in her mind with an impulse so strong she could not even admit it to herself. Her mother's death could not be overlooked, and anger gathered where heartache should claim dominance. However, no tears fell from her eyes. Instead, cancerous cells of hate surged through her veins as she accepted her role as the new Lady Byrne.

Alice comforted her sisters in their time of need.

Agatha accepted her tears along with Cora. They clung to each other and their eldest sister. In her youthful brain, she understood the warning that the flames whispered to her, yet nothing else about the situation made sense. She refused to call out the name. The consequence of doing so avoided her level of comprehension.

Cora straightened up and wiped the tears from her eyes. The pain burned her ribcage from hyperventilating. She went to their mother's side laying a hand on the shroud. "We need to give Mother a proper burial," She said. "She deserves to know we can carry on in her absence. Alice, you bring her out while Aggie and I will build a pyre. We'll blanket her with the flowers that are still in bloom and vines."

A forked tongue tasted the air in the room salivating at the scent of death. Lady Byrne floated out of the house toward the small stack of wood prepared by her children. It's probably more than they could sacrifice as the chill in the air reminded them of the approaching winter. The tongue disappeared behind the succubus's smile from the thin shadows. She hadn't given up on claiming Alice for her new pet. The determination burned in her eyes, a growing intent to possess one of Lady Byrne's precious daughters. If no opportunities arrived for her chance, then she planned to create one. Her willing young vessel would speak the name Agrat bat Mahlat before the veil thinned.

Dusk brought the girls' attention to the task ahead of them. Their bare feet splashed through the damp grass toward the pyre. They took their positions, the younger girls on either side while the oldest sister stood at the head facing the setting sun. Alice led the chant to their god, arms raised above her head. When her arms dropped after the prayer she nodded to Cora.

The middle daughter concentrated hard on the kindling at the center of the pyre. Flames ignited with a pop as the crackling sound from the wood filled the quiet evening. There in the south end of their yard, that's where the girls stood watching their mother's body return to the earth in ashes. Her magic and energy released back to the universe.

Agatha summoned four vine braids to grow over them into a gazebo. The plants branched out reaching for the others until a canopy protected them. She blew a kiss with a wave goodbye. Her sisters watched her start toward the house rubbing at the sleep that made her eyelids heavy. Mental exhaustion won the battle for the day. The emotional stress proved more than she could handle any longer. She dropped her boots in the box by the door walking up to bed without changing into her nightgown. Agatha drifted off in an instant.

Cora stood watching the embers waste down to glowing coals. She crossed her arms close against the cool wind and pain in her chest. An arm slipped around the lower part of her back. Cora saw Alice lay their heads together with the burden placed on their shoulders. The loss of their mother doubled its weight by the responsibility of caring for Agatha. Cora grabbed her sister, sobbing into her shoulder.

"Come on, Cora. Let's go make sure Aggie is okay," Alice said. She led her by the arm toward the open door. "I wonder if she realized that she left it open. I don't even remember when she went inside. Do you?"

Cora shook her head. Her voice failed to respond to any commands. She suffered from the simplest of functions since she started the fire. Every bit of her strength ciphered down her legs leaving them weak and unresponsive. Alice kept her walking to their bedroom where she collapsed on the bed.

Alice kissed her sister on the head while stroking her hair. She turned to Agatha which she did the same. Agatha mumbled something Alice couldn't understand in her dream talk. She sat down on her bed and waited. When she watched Cora close her eyes, she wandered downstairs to prepare for the morning. Drowsiness tickled every nerve with a little more force as time ticked away. She ignored the strain in her eyes and limbs slowing her movements.

Alice fought back a yawn. The clock clicked further past her normal bedtime while she finished the last of the dishes. Wood lay in the fireplace, prepared for the morning fire. She laid the egg basket close to the stove for breakfast, and the pan was left on its burner over the second stack of wood. Alice dropped her scrub brush into the murky bucket with the resolve to dump it after getting some sleep. She stumbled up the stairs passing the room she'd shared with sisters since their birth for the room that belonged to her mother. She curled under the blanket comforted by fading scent on the pillow.

Somewhere in the darkness, Agrat bat Mahlat formulated her plan whispering ideas into the ears of weak men. Men she knew would come up with the most despicable plans imaginable. The succubus licked her lips, lusting for the carnage she wanted to inflict on the children of Lady Byrne for her insubordination. She watched the men writhe in their sleep among their dreams and disgusting fantasies. Agrat bat Mahlat gave a wicked, wicked grin.

Chapter Five

Aggie woke up to an empty bedroom. She rubbed the sleep from her eyes feeling the warmth that wisped into the room. A morning fire complemented the slow heat trapped by the windows in the sunlight. She wandered down the stairs to discover her sisters whispering at the kitchen table. Alice raised a finger to her lips then waved Aggie to join them.

Cora gathered a plate and fork which Alice loaded with breakfast. They took turns kissing their baby sister on the head while she ate. Neither spoke another word as the tension grew thicker. Aggie knew a decision had to be made about what became of them now that Mother was gone. Three girls would remain at their home in Raven Hollow or try to find a way to survive in town. Aggie preferred to stay in this house that she knew and felt safe. The decision belonged to her sisters though. How could they?

The daughters of Lady Byrne sat in the quiet morning with the sound of a crackling fire behind a fork scraping on a plate. The three of them still in their nightgowns refused to accept that chores waited to be finished. A fading voice of their mother gave out the daily assignments until they were left with silence and full awareness of the growing noises outside. They heard the horses approaching long before six townsmen reached the outskirts of the property. Former soldiers of the South warped by violence, injuries, and trauma shared a common goal, to violate the Byrne children.

Each man dropped from his horse chopping at the protective vines with rusted bayonets. A queer smile distorted their faces combined with a fanatical gleam in their eyes. One man wearing a gray Confederate hat aimed his pistol toward the house squeezing the trigger twice. The girls screamed laying down on the porch, arms covered their heads. He pulled at the vines hoping to force his way past them. The screams fueled his rage much to the delight of one creature, Agrat bat Mahlat.

The succubus sacrificed her view from an upper window to slither her way near Alice's ear. She whispered to the eldest daughter, "You only need to say the words, and I'll make it all go away. Say the words, and I'll kill them all. No one will hurt you again."

Alice shook her head. "I can't. I promised my momma. She made me swear to never say them if something happened to her."

"You're a fool!" She hissed. "They're going to kill you, girl. They'll defile your sisters to the point that they pray for death and then murder them too. After they leave your bodies to rot, I'll strip your bones myself!"

The words of the succubus sank in, but Alice's decision fell short of Agrat's plan. "Be gone from this place and never return creature. You'll not cause harm to my sisters or me. You'll never send another soul to carry out your foul deed for you. Do you understand?"

Agrat bat Mahlat felt an invisible shove with the force of a cyclone, which sent her beyond the property into the deadly sunlight. She tried to slither for safety in the shadows to no avail. Her body was pinned in the rays causing her skin to melt away feeling like a burn victim at mercy of boiling oil. She screamed until holes burned into her lungs deflating the once precious air leaving her husk to silent disposal. With the creature's life force gone, Alice turned all her attention to the new threat.

Her energy blocked the next shot aimed in their direction. She stood up in front of her sisters prepared to sacrifice herself to save them. But she had full intentions of taking the disgusting men to hell with her. Alice aimed for the horses causing a small stampede of scrambling beasts.

Curses flowed from the men echoing their frustration. Alice ignored their threats of bodily harm and death. She spoke to her siblings. "Don't worry. I'll keep you safe. Stay low in case they shoot again," she said.

Agatha Byrne refused to let her sister fight alone, barely visible above the porch rail, she stood beside Alice. Aggie took her sister's right hand squeezing it tight. "We fought together before and we will fight together now. Cora, we need your help to show them that we are not weak."

She reached out with her free hand commanding more vines to spring from the ground. Her growing restraints secured the men's arms and legs, even if it was for a short time. The purpose proved evident to her sisters who pushed forward with their abilities. Alice surrounded them in an invisible corral restricting their movements further. Cora gathered all her strength blasting them to cinders in the largest inferno she had ever attempted.

The flames burned hot enough to kill them before a scream left their throats. Alice closed the energy field causing the fire to disappear leaving charcoal statues. Alice walked closer to the remains with her bare feet slipping through the wet grass. The ends of her gown darkened from the gathered dew even as she stopped twenty feet from the dead men. "We are always strongest when we fight together."

She whispered to the earth her plans to embrace each dead body with a plant coffin covered in thorns. She wrapped their heads in crowns as a final touch not noticing her sisters had joined her to watch the creations grow. Aggie reached for their hands. "After all, we are the witches of Raven Hollow."

Raymond G. Newsome is a multi-genre author, whose books are available worldwide. His works include Rise of the Fallen (Dark Fantasy), I am Brian (Serial Killer Thriller), and The Adventures of Pipsqueak and Bob (Children's Adventure).